Best Christmas Ever

DEANN SOLEIL

Cover Designer: Covers by Sophie

Editor: Staceys Bookcorner Editing Services

Contents

Content Warnings

- Co-workers to lovers
- One bed
- Age gap (28/35)
- Work trip adventure
- Bondage with tinsel
- Ice play
- Spanking with candy cane shaped paddle
- Candy cane vibrator
- Blindfold use
- Santa hat vibrator
- Use of nipple clamps
- Glass candy cane butt plug
- He cleans her up
- Oral giving/receiving
- Sex toy company employees
- Interracial relationship
- Holiday novella

Blurb:

Ava expected another ordinary day at the office full of the usual sales work, until an email from her boss changes everything.

The company is in need of volunteers to test out their new collection of holiday toys.

She's immediately intrigued, but she has one choice to make. Should she take on the task alone, or invite the man she's been wanting for months...

Demetrius Miles.

The charming man a few desks away.

How far can she go until the professional line becomes too blurred to see?

Playlist

Burning Blue - Mariah the Scientist
On Sight - Coco Jones
Hearts on Deck - Ella Mai
Worst Behaviour- Kwn (Feat. Kehlani)
Made for Me- Muni Long
I Need Her- Bryson Tiller
Ectasy (Remix) - Ciara & Normani (Feat. Teyana Taylor)
This Christmas- Chris Brown
Winter Dreams - Kelly Clarkson
Sweater Weather - Penatonix
This Winter - Kevin Ross
Try a Little Tenderness- Chris Brown

CHAPTER 1
Ava

Growing up I always knew that I wanted to do something in the business arena, so I decided to get my bachelor's degree and start the search for a job. It was always hard knowing exactly what I wanted to do, but when I started my self-exploration journey, I learned about Lustful Vibe.

It's been five years since I began my career as a sex toy sales associate, and I love every part of it. I am able to help people find the perfect product to satisfy their needs, whether they're just getting into using them or want to learn more. This job has been so rewarding, and it gives me something to look forward to when I go to the office.

When I woke up this morning, I felt refreshed and I knew it was going to be a good day. I go through my usual routine to make myself look presentable and make my way to work.

After a ten-minute drive, I settle at my desk, checking my emails, when I see an email from our boss, Benjamin.

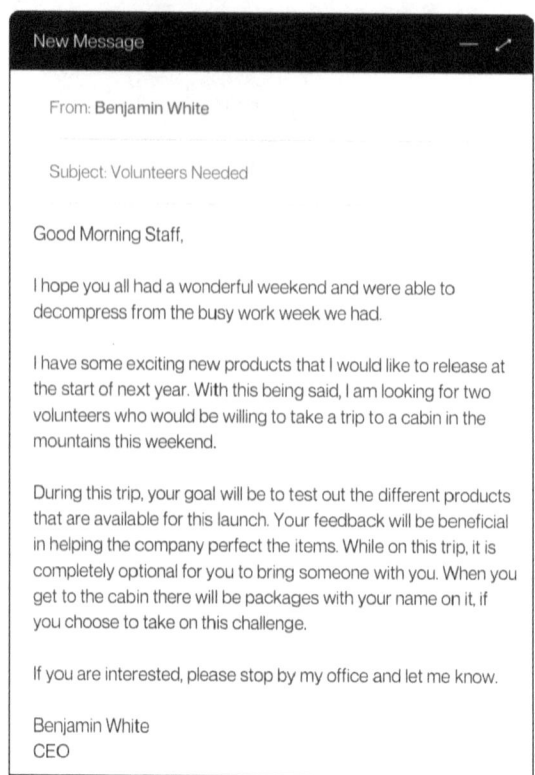

This looks like a good opportunity that I don't think I want to pass up. With Juliana being on the design team at work and my best friend, I'm surprised she didn't tell me about these new products that are up for testing. I typically get the early information from her, so I can be on the lookout for when they come out.

Before I get too focused on the email and what it would look like to be a volunteer for this opportunity, I decide to go make a coffee. I love starting my day with a

French vanilla coffee with one pack of sugar in it—it always hits the spot for me.

As I make my way to where the coffee machine is located, in the community area of the company, Juliana stops me to chat.

"Hey, did you see the email from Benjamin this morning?"

"I did. I am actually interested in being a volunteer for it. This would be a good opportunity for me to try out some products before I start selling them," I say before I am cut off.

"Good morning, ladies," Benjamin says with a smile on his face.

I don't see how this man can be so happy with all the stress he has to deal with behind the scenes to ensure the products are relevant and good to sell. Maybe it is because he put out the volunteer email, or maybe he just enjoys being in our presence.

I wouldn't mind hooking up with the boss, but I have my eyes on one of my co-workers—Demetrius Miles.

He has the brightest smile, a full beard that connects with his mustache, brown eyes, and muscles that define his arms. The things I would do to him has me getting giddy, but I know I need to focus my attention back on Benjamin.

"Good morning, boss. It's weird seeing you down here this early in the morning, normally you are up in your office taking care of business," I say.

"Well, I was just wandering around, seeing if I had

any takers for the trip to the cabin. Have y'all had a chance to check it out?"

I should have known this was why he came down here.

"I checked it out but can Juliana and I have a little more time to chat and figure out if this is the right option. If it is, then we will let you know."

Juliana shares a few words with Benjamin, and he nods in agreement before he makes his way back to the elevator, and back to his office.

Over the next five minutes, Juliana and I continue to chat. She fills me in on how these products are a surprise to her. With her having a close friendship with one of our toy makers James, she often gets the insight scoop of what toys are coming. This time he didn't mention this new collection coming out.

She does share the same excitement as me, and we decide we should give it a try. There's no harm in trying out these products and being able to chat about them with not only my colleague, but my best friend.

After we make the decision to participate, we head to Benjamin's office together. He immediately sees us and waves us in before we have to knock on the door.

"That was a fast talk. I thought y'all would need more time," he says.

This man always has to make some sort of comment when they just aren't necessary. Juliana chimes in and shares some words with Benjamin that catches him by surprise.

"Are you sure you sent the email out to everyone in the company because it seems like you were waiting on what we would say about it," I let out. He hesitates for a moment which gives me all the answers that I need to know. "I take that as a no, it was only to us then."

"Maybe that is true, but I knew you both would be perfect for the job because of your passion for this company and the skills that you bring forward."

"Hmm, okay. Well count us in. When do we get started?"

"Immediately. I want you both to head out and go pack for the weekend. You saw the details in the email, but I will text you both the address of the cabin. I hope y'all have fun. Be sure to write down the good, the bad, and the ugly for the toys that you try out. I want it all."

I bet he does want it all. He wants to know exactly how it makes us feel. *Shit, does he need to know how many orgasms we have, too*? We will see what he ends up getting.

He goes on to explain how this is a surprise drop that has a focus on holiday-themed sex toys, which makes this even more exciting. Juliana and I are both in agreement for continuing to participate in this project.

We make our way back to our desks and grab our items and head out to pack. "I will see you in a little bit," I say.

CHAPTER 2

Ava

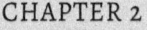

While I head to my car, I think about how it could be important to let Demetrius know that I will be out of the office for the rest of the day and the weekend. I work with him all the time, so we like to keep each other updated on when we are out just in case any important information comes up. With him being a data analyst for the company I can often check-in with him to see how my sales are doing compared to others who are in the organization.

I am happy to say that I am ranked number one in sales within our company. I have busted my ass every day to get to where I am, so I make sure that I am still on top of my game.

Sometimes I am able to get reassurance that I am a great asset to this organization when I feel like I am not doing my best, or when I am just struggling with life in general. Ultimately, I decide to go ahead and text him just to check-in.

> Me: Hey, I was presented with an exciting opportunity so I will be out of the office today and the rest of the weekend.

I hear my phone ding immediately, but I decide to wait to look at what he says until I get home. I turn up the music and listen to some country as I make the ten-minute drive back home.

WHEN I ARRIVE AT MY HOUSE, I LOOK DOWN AT my phone and see what Demetrius said.

> Him: You going to leave me hanging or are you going to tell me what this opportunity is?

Hmm should I tell him what happened or just leave it how it is.

After I get into the house, I decide to FaceTime him to make things easier. After a few rings, his handsome face comes into view.

"You miss me already that you had to see my face?" he says as he answers the phone.

"You wish. I just thought it would be easier to call you and touch base about what is going on."

"Ava, you do realize you don't always have to keep me updated on your festivities unless you want me to be a part of it, right?"

I take a pause to think about why I want to see his face and why it is important that I am giving him this update right now. Maybe it is because I have some feelings deep down for him, or maybe as co-workers it is important to have these conversations. I really don't know.

"How about you just get used to the calls. I know you enjoy hearing what is going on."

"Well, go on then, don't leave me hanging over here."

"Let's just say I get paid to have some holiday fun while I am on company time." He begins to gesture for me to continue talking, so I do. "I get to test out some of the newest holiday toys. Benjamin is sending me and Juliana to a cabin where we will have a box waiting for us to unpack with who knows what inside it."

"That sounds like it will be a good time. You need any help?" he asks with a wink.

"Nope. I need to go see what it's all about. Maybe if you get lucky then I will reach out for your help, but don't get your hopes up."

"I gotta get back to work but keep me posted on how everything goes and if you need me. Have a great weekend."

"Will do. Have a great rest of your day at work."

I hang up, feeling giddy. I can't believe I told him what the weekend will consist of. Part of me wants him there with me to help test out these toys, but I also don't want to make my feelings known too soon.

I guess I will find out what I need once I get there and if I really need him or not.

CHAPTER 3
Demetrius

There is something about Ava that gets me every time. She lights up the office with her contagious personality and smile. I will say that I am lucky to be able to work hand-in-hand with her and making sure she continues to excel in the company.

When she decided to call me today, it was a little shocking. It is rare that we do video calls because that seems too personal for colleagues. Typically, we are either doing a regular call, or we will text.

Knowing that she is going to be in a cabin testing sex toys has me picturing the way her body will come undone with each one. I am a little jealous that I wasn't able to get an official invite. I really hope once she gets there she will realize that she wants me to help her out.

I've been keeping my feelings for her to myself. I would love to be able to tell her that I am crushing on her, but I don't want to make things weird for us since we work so closely together. Maybe if she determines that she wants me there with her this weekend, then I can ease my way into telling her how I feel.

Worst case scenario, I lose one of my close colleagues. Best case scenario, I walk away with someone to call my own. I really hope it will work out under the best-case scenario. I know we would be a good match for one another. We are both driven, bubbly, and motivated to do our best with any task that we are faced with. I think that means we would be able to work things out for a long-term relationship.

With it being a few nights before Christmas, I keep picturing what it will look like if I confess my feelings to her on Christmas Eve or even the actual holiday date. We would be by the fireplace, cuddled up with hot chocolate watching holiday movies. I can see her dressed comfortably with her hair up in a messy bun, reciprocating my feelings after I tell her how I feel first.

Well, I wish that's what would happen.

A man can only hope and dream for what is to come. I just need to make it happen, but until then I need to focus on work. I have to finalize the quarterly report, so the company can see which toys are successful and which ones we need to get rid of next year. I will say this is my least favorite part of the job, but I know I can get it done.

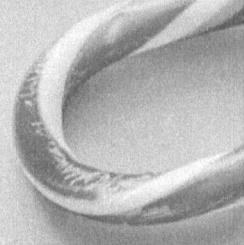

CHAPTER 4
Ava

O nce I got off the phone with Demetrius, I was able to get everything packed up and ready to go for the weekend. I really don't know what to expect, but I am pretty excited. At first, I thought it would be weird doing this with Juliana but since we are so close it doesn't feel weird at all.

The good thing about this whole situation is when I looked up the cabin, I noticed it is really big. This will ensure that we pick rooms on different sides of the house to not be able to hear what is going on with one another.

I know there is no rush to get to the cabin because I have some time, but I decide to hop in my car and send Juliana a text so I can go get acclimated.

Me: I am heading to the cabin. I
should be there in about twenty
minutes.

> Juliana: I am leaving my house in five minutes so I will get there a little after you.

> Me: Sounds good. I will see you soon. Drive safe.

> Juliana: You, too.

I scroll through my music playlist and pick my R&B one, so I can listen to some of the new hits while I make my drive. Once I hit play, I attach my phone to the magnetic holder in my car air vent and get driving.

AFTER MY TWENTY-MINUTE DRIVE TO THE cabin, I get to the outside and recognize it looks a lot bigger than I'd anticipated. The pictures definitely didn't do it any justice. I put my car in park, grab my suitcase, and make my way to the front door. I put in the door code and head inside to pick which room I want. That's the perks of getting somewhere first—you get first dibs.

As I walk around the cabin, I realize there is a fireplace in the living room, a spacious kitchen, a hot tub in the backyard, and four bedrooms. Two of the bedrooms have one of the big jacuzzi tubs in it with an electric fireplace, so I am definitely opting for one of those. I choose the one on the far right of the house. It's always been a habit since I grew up to be on the right side of the house, so I have just continued to do it as an adult.

When I put all of my things in the bedroom, I peruse the bathroom. I am obsessed! Mine has double shower heads in it. That has always been a dream of mine, but I have never had the opportunity to get them installed where I live. I know I will definitely be taking advantage of using them while I am here. After I finish taking a look around, I head to the living room where I notice two boxes. One labeled Ava and one labeled Juliana.

This is going to be fun.

Even though I am tempted into opening my box, I refrain and wait for Juliana. During the cooler weather I always enjoy a glass of mulled wine, so I pull out the kettle and throw some wine in there to get warm. There is just something about wine being warm that just makes my body feel good. Hopefully, it will be done by the time Juliana gets here.

About ten minutes later, I hear the code being entered into the front door. Juliana swings open the door, and she has a face of excitement for what we are getting ourselves into. "Hey girl, I'm going to go look around and find my room."

A couple minutes later she heads back into the kitchen like she is in search of something, but the moment she eyes the bottle of wine next to the kettle she pours herself a glass.

"It's not really warm yet," I say, but she doesn't seem to care. She pours herself a glass and grabs me one as well. Once she appears to be satisfied with the taste, she comes over and joins me on the couch.

"Is there something you want to tell me? You seem like something is bothering you."

"It's just been a really long week already, plus I've been thinking about how I'm tired of being lonely for the holidays. I feel like I need a companion to keep me company, so maybe this opportunity will open the doors for that."

"I think this is a good opportunity. We will see what happens."

Her eyes immediately go to the boxes with our names on them.

"What are we waiting for? Let's open them," she says.

"Alright, let's do it," I say with excitement in my tone.

Slowly, I undo the bow that is sitting on the top of the box. When I throw it aside and get the box open, I can feel my jaw drop. *What the fuck am I getting myself into.* There are some interesting looking items in here. I love how they are all holiday themed, but some of this stuff I don't know how I am going to be able to use alone. I sure as hell won't be asking Juliana to help me with them, so I might need to ask Demetrius to come.

"Umm, I think these items are meant for us to do in private and not together. I mean unless you really want to," I say with a laugh that causes her to bust out laughing as well.

"I love you, but I don't think so. I think this could be my opportunity to invite Collin from work to have a little fun with."

Juliana genuinely seems like she is in a better mood with getting everything off her chest. I love how we are able to joke around and laugh with one another, especially when it comes to something like sex toys. I don't think I would want to choose anyone else to be my best friend. I also don't think anyone else would handle this unboxing the same way as we are. Truly, I'm glad our boss put us up for this task because I couldn't have done it with anyone else.

"I think I might text Demetrius and ask him to come join me. If you don't mind?"

"Girl, you know damn well I don't mind. I have wanted to see the two of you together for a while now. Plus if Collin says yes to coming, then it will be perfect."

"I have just been so scared to tell him how I really feel about him. Maybe this will be a steppingstone in the right direction though. What if he tries to break me while he is here? I can only imagine what he is carrying in his pants."

"I don't want to picture that. He's all yours, girl. Just reach out and see what he thinks. I'm sure he will jump on that opportunity."

I listen to her and send the text.

> Me: Remember what we talked about earlier? Well, I think I might need a little more help than I thought I would.

> Demetrius: Say less. Send me the details and I can be there tomorrow.

Fuck, this man is eager.

Juliana looks over at his response and starts smiling. "See. Told you."

"Yeah, yeah, yeah. I will send him the deets but let's relax, have some wine, and maybe watch a movie."

"I think I want to go for a walk to clear my head and call Collin to see if he wants to come for the weekend."

"It's getting dark out there, so be safe and call me if you need me. I do think it's a good idea to invite him over, so you're not being a third wheel."

"I'm sure it will be good too," she says as she throws on her jacket.

When she gets ready to head out, I send Demetrius a text back.

> Me: Well damn, I didn't have to do any begging for you to come

> Demetrius: I mean who would pass up an opportunity like this with a beautiful woman

Ahh this man just called me beautiful. Let me keep it casual.

> Me: If you say so. Just come tomorrow. The address is: 1500 Carroway Lane

> Demetrius: Oh, I will definitely come tomorrow 😉

I literally can't with this man. I decide not to engage, grabbing a glass of mulled wine, and heading to take a shower with those dual shower heads.

CHAPTER 5

Demetrius

I can't tell if I scared Ava off or not by my text messages, but it just felt so good to say. Her leaving me on read does make me wonder if she really wants me to come or not, but since she gave me the address, I think it will be fine.

She told me to come tomorrow, but I really don't feel like it. I am just going to pop up and surprise her. What's wrong with an extra night of being together? I know I don't see a problem with it. I grab some clothes for the weekend and throw them in my suitcase along with the toiletries I'm going to need.

I take a quick shower and make sure I smell good before I hop in the car and make the fifteen-minute drive to the cabin. On my way, I stop and grab a bouquet of sunflowers because I know it's one of her favorite flowers. Her desk is decorated with them at work.

I really don't know how she is going to react, but I hope it will be a good reaction.

When I arrive at the cabin, I send Ava a text.

> Me: You should open the cabin door.

It takes a few minutes but my phone buzzes with a text from her.

> Ava: Why would I do that?

> Me: Because you want to see my face.

I don't know if she really wants to see my face or not, but it sounded like a good response in the moment. After what feels like forever, I see Ava open the front door. She is in holiday-themed pajamas looking cuter than ever.

I hop out the car and grab my suitcase from the backseat before making my way to the front door.

"Didn't I tell you to come tomorrow?" she asks.

"Yeah, you did, but what is the fun in waiting another night when I could be here tonight."

"Whatever you say. Just get in here before you freeze."

I step into the cabin, but Ava steps outside and looks around like she is looking for something.

"Is everything good?" I ask.

"Kinda. Juliana went out for a walk, and I thought she would be back by now, but she isn't so I'm a little worried about her."

"I'm sure she is okay. You should send her a text to make sure."

I take a peek over at her phone as she types out a message:

> Ava: Just checking on you. I was thinking about heading to sleep soon. Also, Demetrius doesn't know what tomorrow means. He popped up tonight.

Almost instantly her phone dings.

> Juliana: Why doesn't that surprise me. Collin doesn't listen either. He told me he is coming tonight too. Go ahead and head to bed, I will be back soon.

"See she is fine. You're just overreacting. Can you show me around?"

"Maybe I was a little," she lets out a chuckle. "But yeah, I can show you around."

With that, we start to take a walk around the cabin and stop in the kitchen to grab a glass of mulled wine and turn off the kettle. Then she shows me the room is she is staying in.

"This is where we will be. I hope you don't snore. Some of us like to get an actual good night's sleep," she says with a laugh.

"You don't have to worry about that. I would like to think I sleep quietly and won't disturb you."

"Good. Now if you don't mind, I'm going to get into bed and watch a scary movie."

"You had me at scary. Let's do it."

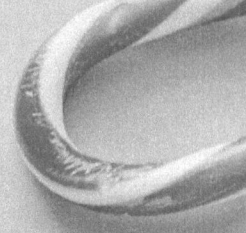

CHAPTER 6
Ava

Him coming a day early is a complete surprise, but a good one. I was getting worried about being here alone with Juliana going for a walk, so now I don't have to worry about that.

When we get comfortable in bed to watch the movie, Juliana sends me a text.

> Juliana: I'm back. Collin pulled up at the same time as me too. I hope you sleep well.

> Me: Good, don't have too much fun tonight. 😊 I hope you sleep well, too!

I put my phone on the nightstand, and we pick a random scary movie to watch. I can feel Demeterius's arms close to my body. Part of me wishes he would just wrap them around me and pull me in closer, but I know I can't make that known right now. He just got here, so I can't scare him off right away. If I do, then I might not be able to accomplish the tasks that my boss gave me for testing out the toys.

Instead of thinking about the what if's, I draw my attention onto the screen.

ALMOST TWO HOURS LATER, THE MOVIE IS DONE and I absolutely loved it. There was so much gore in it, which is right up my alley for picking a scary movie.

"Did you like the movie?" I ask Demetrius.

"Yeah, it wasn't bad. I think we should do this more often."

"How about we focus on what I need to do for our boss first. If you do a good job helping me out, then maybe we can talk about what happens after we leave here."

"Fine. I will do what you ask me to."

"Good, now I'm heading to bed."

I turn over, throw my eye mask on, and drift off to sleep.

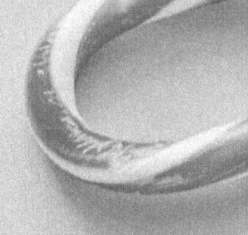

CHAPTER 7
Ava
FRIDAY: DECEMBER 21ST

I wake up and feel big hands wrapped around my body. I have no idea how we got to this point because we were definitely not facing the same way when we went to sleep. His hands around my body does provide some comfort to me, so I don't want this to end. I think Demetrius can tell I'm awake now because he instantly pulls his hands away from me.

"Good morning, beautiful," Demetrius says from behind me.

"When you see my face and hair, you definitely won't be thinking that," I say with a laugh.

"How about you show me then?"

Oof. I know he is going to regret asking me to do that. I pull my eye mask off my face and put it back down on my nightstand before flipping towards him.

"I don't know why you talk bad about yourself. You still look beautiful, even when you first wake up," he says.

"Well, thank you."

We sit there for a second looking into each other's eyes when I lean in and kiss him.

"Fuck," I mutter softly.

I instantly get up and run out of the room to hide my embarrassment for what just happened. I can't believe I kissed him outside of the toy testing. That was definitely not supposed to happen.

When I get to the kitchen, I see Juliana and Collin are already up making coffee.

"Good morning Ava, how'd you sleep?" Juliana asks.

"Not bad. How about y'all?"

"Pretty good. It's nice around here from what I've seen so far," Collin says.

Not too long after we all catch up Demetrius comes into the room and pours himself a cup of coffee.

"How does everyone feel about going to get some lunch and go snow tubing later?" Demetrius asks.

"I'm down, if y'all are," Juliana asks, looking between Collin and I.

"Let's do it," I say, while Collin nods in agreement.

"Well let's go get ourselves together and meet back up in the living room," Collin says.

With it already being 10:30 a.m., I decide to head to get ready, Demetrius following behind me.

I get into the bathroom and start to brush my teeth to avoid any conversation with him because I'm a little nervous to spend alone time together throughout the weekend. This is the first time we will be together like this, so I need to adjust. I think he gets the hint because he brushes his at the same time as me. Once we are done, I turn to put my clothes on, but before I can get out of the bathroom, he pins me where my back is against the sink.

"We should talk about what happened. You can't avoid me forever. We have all weekend together," he says.

"I don't really know what there is to say. My body had a mind of its own."

He gets closer and whispers into my ear, "Are you sure you didn't want the kiss to happen?"

I can feel chills running down my spine. Maybe I did want it to happen, but why would I admit that. I try to respond, but instead he pulls me in and kisses me deeply.

Fuck. This feels so wrong, but so right.

I want to push him away, but I don't. I lean into the kiss instead. He picks me up and places me on the bathroom sink as we continue to kiss. His hands start to wander along my body when I let out, "We can't do this right now. We have to get ready to go to lunch with Juliana and Collin."

I can see the disappointment grow across his face. "Fine, but when we get back tonight, I don't know if I will be able to keep my hands off of you."

"That is the point. We do have some toys to try out later." I let out a laugh.

He kisses me one more time before pulling me down from the sink. "You're right about that."

Once I'm back on my feet, I fix my hair and throw on some comfortable clothes for the rest of the day's festivities.

AFTER WE FINISH GETTING READY, WE HEAD back to the kitchen where Juliana and Collin are waiting for us on the couch.

"Alright, let's head to the snow tubing resort and get food there," I say.

Demetrius decides to drive so we don't have to take multiple vehicles. I slide into the passenger seat while Juliana and Collin get in the back. The resort is only five minutes from here, so it is a quick and easy drive.

When we arrive at the resort, Demetrius comes over and opens my door for me.

What a gentleman.

"You know I can open my own door, right?" I ask.

"I know you can, but I want to do it."

Juliana gives me a knowing look like I should just let him be the man he is and not complain. Maybe I just should.

Juliana and Collin lead the way into the restaurant. "Table for four, please," she says.

Within seconds we are being escorted to one of the booths by the window. The waitress comes over and grabs our drink order while we peruse through the menu. I think I am going to do brunch since I'm feeling like having some eggs.

A few minutes later, the waitress returns with the drinks and takes our orders.

"I'm pretty excited that I get to spend the day with my best friend and y'all guys," I say.

"I was actually surprised when I got the invite to come, but I'm sure it will be a good time," Collin says.

"Did Juliana fill you in on what the weekend entails because you're in for a surprise if not," Demetrius asks Collin.

Before he can respond, Juliana cuts in. "Nope, I wanted it to be a surprise for him."

I let out a laugh, "oh, he's definitely in for a surprise alright."

We all keep making small talk while we wait for our food to arrive. With Collin working at Lustful Vibe, I'm sure he will be just fine with the way the weekend goes. I just hope he doesn't hurt my bestie and actually brings her the joy she needs this holiday season.

I get pulled from my thoughts when the waitress comes back and starts handing out food. "Scrambled eggs with cheese, sausage links, and hashbrowns," she says as she places the plate in front of me. This is pretty much my go-to meal whenever I get breakfast foods. We each enjoy our food before getting ready for the next activity of the day.

CHAPTER 8

Ava

We all finish eating our food around the same time and boy was it good. Most days I opt for a protein shake because I don't have time to eat a full meal, but I will definitely be getting more for here on out.

"Alright y'all, ready to head snowtubing?" I ask.

They all nod in agreement, so we walk to the next building over to get checked in. I haven't been before, so I am a little nervous but it seems like it won't be too bad.

"There will be someone at the top and the bottom of the hill at all times to ensure that you are good to go. You can either do the tube as a single or a double, the choice is yours. Be sure to have fun, but do not intentionally knock other people off the tubes. Does anyone have any questions for me?" the lady at the register says as she puts our wristbands on.

We look at each other and nobody appears to have any questions.

"If there are no questions, then go enjoy."

When we get outside to where the tubes are, I notice

there is a moving walkway that we get on to get to the top of the hill to start our snowtubing. I decide for my first time to do a single tube to get the hang of it.

It feels like the moving walkway takes forever for us to get to the top, but when we are finally up there, I get really nervous.

"Hey beautiful, is everything okay?" Demetrius asks.

"I'm just a little nervous since I've never done this before."

"Take your time, you got this. If it makes you feel more comfortable we can hold hands going down the hill?"

I contemplate if that is the right decision to make or not and ultimately decide we should do it.

"Okay, let's do it."

We both get into our snow tubes, grab hands, and push off to make our way down the hill. The adrenaline is hitting me in a good way. I hyped myself up for nothing because it isn't bad at all.

When we get to the bottom of the hill we get out of our tubes and I cheer with excitement. "I did it! Thank you so much for holding my hand through it."

He leans in for a kiss. "I will always be here to hold your hand if you want me to."

Juliana sees the kiss and she winks at me. I shake my head to let her know it isn't what it looks like but she just laughs and she makes her way back to the tubes.

"Can we do the double tube this time?" I ask Demetrius.

"Let's do it. I can grab the tube for us."

We make our way to the top of the hill again and I

position myself in front of him in the tube. "Here we go," he says as he pushes off.

I think this is the most fun I have had in a long time.

AN HOUR GOES BY AND WE GET READY TO HEAD back to the cabin to test out our first toy of the night.

"I had a great time with y'all today. It was fun being able to try new experiences and make new memories," I say when we get into the car.

"I agree," Juliana replies.

We make our way back to the cabin and we all decide to part ways for the rest of the night.

CHAPTER 9

Demetrius

When we get back to the cabin, I grab a bottle of wine, two wine glasses, and two water bottles from the fridge to bring back to the bedroom with us.

"Do you want to hop into the hot tub, catch up on how things have been going and figure out a plan for this weekend?" I ask.

She contemplates for a minute. "I don't have a bathing suit with me."

"I don't either. I'm getting in with my boxers on."

"I'm down then, too."

She starts to strip off her clothes until she is left in a matching panty and bra set. I look her up and down and I can't help but bite my lip at the sight I'm seeing in front of me. I slowly make my way closer to her.

"Your body is amazing," I say as I wrap my hands around her waist, pulling her in for a kiss.

She pulls away and says, "We're supposed to be getting in the hot tub, remember?"

"I remember, but first I want to get a little taste of what I'm working with tonight."

I start to plant kisses along her neck as she lets out a soft moan. I slowly lower myself down to my knees, as I continue trailing kisses along her body. I look up and see her head falling back with pleasure.

I slowly move her panties to the side and take a quick lap at her center. *Fuck, she tastes so sweet.* I start to pick up my pace and lick in between her folds causing her to moan out my name.

"Demetrius."

"Yes, beautiful?"

"I think that's enough for right now. Let's head to the hot tub," she says in between moans.

"Fine, if that's what you want," I say as I take one more long lap at her center. I move her panties back over.

"Let's go. I will get us a glass of wine," I say.

I pour us each a glass of wine and we make our way out to the hot tub.

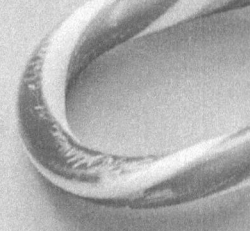

CHAPTER 10
Ava

Fuck, the way that man just devoured my pussy has me in for something tonight. When we get to the hot tub I can see some remnants of my wetness in his beard so I lean over and wipe it off.

"You have a little something in your beard," I say.

"I bet I do. Your pussy was dripping for me just then. Wait until we head back into the room to test out the first toy, you're really going to want more."

"Don't be so cocky. We will see what happens."

I'm sure he is right but I can't let him see my weakness and give in to what I'm saying right away. We have to build up to that, but I will say, I'm so ready to see what hides behind his boxers, but I know I need to wait.

"Answer something for me," he says.

"What is it?" Confusion fills my face.

"Why did you choose me to come this weekend to help you out?"

Hmm... do I give him the real reason or do I keep

that to myself. I feel like I should be honest, but I wasn't trying to get into all of that, this early on.

"Do you want the real reason or do you want the reason I have been making up in my mind?"

"How about this... I take a guess. If I'm right, we head back inside, hop in the shower, and finish what we started."

"And if you get it wrong?"

"If I get it wrong then we will just continue to hang out in the hot tub until you're ready." He reaches out his hand to shake on it.

"Deal," I say while shaking his hand back.

CHAPTER 11

Demetrius

I inch my way closer to her in the hot tub where my mouth is just inches away from her ear.

"What I think is you have some underlying feelings for me, that you are afraid to admit." I can see her cheeks flush with embarrassment at my assumption. "Don't be afraid to embrace the way you feel," I say while pulling her to straddle on my lap.

"And what if you're right?" she asks while looking into my eyes.

"If I'm right, then maybe I will admit that I feel the same way back."

There is an instant flip in her when she brings her mouth to my lips, kissing me deeply.

"Maybe we should bring this back to the room," I say in between kisses.

She instantly lifts herself off of me and makes her way out of the hot tub while reaching for my hand to follow. With no second guessing, I grab her hand back and follow her out into the room.

"Let's hop in the shower to get cleaned off from the hot tub," she says.

We make our way into the shower where she slowly removes her bra and panties causing my eyes to wander up and down her body.

"You're so beautiful, Ava."

Everything about her body is just sticking out to me. From the way her nipples harden with the sound of her name to the way she is trying to slow her breathing down.

I slowly pull down my boxers and her eyes immediately find their way to my dick.

"Fuck," she mutters.

"Do you like what you see or something," I question with a laugh.

"Shush it. Let's get this shower over with," she says.

We take a quick shower together before we make our way back to the bedroom. I grab the box of toys that is located in the corner of the room and we look through the contents together.

"Let's start with something simple," she says as she grabs the tinsel, blindfold, and candy cane paddle.

Ahh, she's starting with some easy items that can get her warmed up for what I have in store for her this weekend. I want it to be a weekend that she isn't going to forget.

"Well, this is going to be fun. I hope you are fine with giving up a little control tonight because I will definitely be tying you up with that tinsel. We can start slow, though."

She looks at me like she is a little nervous for what is to come.

"If at any point there is something that you don't want to do, please let me know. What safe word do you want to use to indicate where your limits are?"

I can see a sense of relief wash over her with the option to have a way out.

"Cover."

"Did you just say cover? As in a cover on a book?"

"Yup. It was the first thing that popped up in my mind," she says with a laugh.

"Alright, well cover it is, then. Let's start off easy. Bend over the bed with your stomach flat on the bed." She does as I say. "I'm going to start off soft and place two gentle spanks on your ass."

Spank. Spank.

"That wasn't bad. How about you do it harder?" she requests.

I do as she asks and hit her a little harder this time.

Spank. Spank. I can see the way her ass is turning red, as she moans out with each hit.

"You still doing good?" I ask.

"Please do it harder."

I listen to her request and spank her harder causing her to moan out.

"See that wasn't bad at all. I want to try something with you if you're willing to. It isn't a part of the items provided to us, but I want to see how your body reacts to it."

"Okay," she says with hesitation in her voice.

I throw on some sweatpants and say, "I'll be right back."

CHAPTER 12

Ava

I'm sitting waiting and wondering what Demetrius wanted to try as he heads out of the room. I know I shouldn't get in my thoughts, but I am a little nervous about how he feels about my body. I have always been self-conscious about the way I look, so I hope he isn't lying when he told me I'm beautiful. Before I go down the rabbit hole of negative thoughts, Demetrius comes back into the room holding a bowl of ice.

"What the hell do you think you're doing with the ice?"

"Do you trust me?"

"I do, but I'm still curious. I've never seen ice used before in moments such as this one."

"Beautiful, you have nothing to worry about. If things become a bit too much then use your safe word."

"Okay. Will do," I say with some hesitation in my tone.

He takes the tinsel and binds my hands together

above my head, ties my legs to the bed to keep them open, then places the blindfold over my eyes.

"This is going to be a little cold, but I will go slow," he says.

He takes the first piece of ice and begins to bring it down my neck to my chest and then to my nipples. I let out a small moan. The coldness that I feel sends chills through my body, but in a good way. After spending a couple seconds on my nipples he grabs a new piece of ice and drags it down my body to my clit.

"Fuck," I moan out as the ice hits me.

"You good?" he asks.

"I'm more than good," I say.

I think the fact that I can't see or use my hands, is making this more interesting because my body is on high alert for what is to come next. Just when I think he is done I feel his tongue lap at my clit.

"You taste so good."

He begins to pick up his pace and before I know it, I feel two of his fingers slide into me.

"Demetrius," I moan out.

He begins to thrust his fingers in and out of me quickly causing my moans to get louder. As he fucks me with his fingers, I can feel another piece of ice rub against my nipples.

This man is killing me.

Between the ice, his mouth, and his fingers my body is losing it. I can feel my legs begin to tremble at the touch before an orgasm takes over me.

"Fuck, Demetrius. I've never come so fast before."

"I love the way your body reacts to me," he says as he unties my legs from the bed.

It feels good to have some freedom for my legs, but I'm not used to my hands being restricted.

"I want to fuck this sweet pussy of yours."

"Do it then."

With that permission, I can hear a condom wrapper open before he climbs on the bed and lifts my legs up onto his shoulders.

He slowly inserts himself in me and I feel so full.

"You're so big," I let out with a moan.

"Baby girl, I'm not all the way in yet."

Shit, how much more is there to go? It's almost as if he can read my mind when he pushes himself all the way into me, causing a yelp to come out. I can feel him instantly pull out of me as he lifts the blindfold from my eyes.

"Did I hurt you?" he asks with panic in his tone.

"I'm sorry, I didn't mean to yelp. It was just a lot at that moment. Please fuck me."

With that, he instantly pounds into me. Picking up his pace with every stroke. "You're so tight," he says in between thrusts.

I can see that look on his face like he is about to cum. I wish I could wrap my arms around him, but my hands are trapped with the tinsel.

He thrusts harder and before I know it, I can feel his dick throbbing inside of me. He sits there inside of me for a second, then hops off the bed to remove the condom.

I sit there for a second trying to catch my breath as he unties the tinsel from my hands.

"Well damn," he says as he comes to lay next to me.

"That was amazing. I haven't been fucked like that before. I'm definitely keeping you around," I say with a laugh.

I know I don't want him to go anywhere.

"You have me all weekend to do whatever you please with."

Something about that flips a switch in me and makes me upset. I turn so he can't see my face as tears well up in my eyes. I don't know why I'm reacting this way. I just had an amazing time with him, so I shouldn't be feeling this way.

CHAPTER 13
Demetrius

I haven't been able to experiment with a woman before in the ways I just did with Ava. The way her body responded to me had me coming before I wanted to. I know this is going to be a good weekend, especially if I'm able to continue to explore her body in this way.

As we are laying in the bed talking about how we have all weekend to explore, I can tell I struck a nerve. She instantly turns away from me, but I can hear the sniffles coming from her.

I stand up and walk over to her side of the bed.

"Baby girl, did I do something?" I ask as I lift up her chin so we can look at each other.

I can see the tears rolling down her face.

"I'm sorry, I don't know what is wrong with me. I love what we just did and can't wait to see how the rest of the weekend goes, but I kinda want this to go somewhere after the weekend is over. Maybe we can talk about it tomorrow?"

This is not how the night can end. We have to talk it

out or do something about it. I definitely don't want things to be awkward between us the rest of the weekend, especially when we will be spending a lot of time together.

"I really don't want to hurt you and I don't want to end the night on a bad note. I had a great time tonight and I'm looking forward to what else is to come. Is there a way that I can make it up to you before we go to bed?"

I can see the contemplation coming across her face.

"Demetrius, everything is okay. Let's just sleep it off and we can talk tomorrow. I promise I'm going to be fine. It's just been a long day, so I think some sleep will be good. I'm going to go to the bathroom and then lay back down for the night," she says as she gets up and makes her way to the bathroom.

Something about this isn't sitting well with me, but if she says that she is fine, then I'm going to trust that's how she feels. I can't push her into talking about this, but I will be here to cuddle her all night. I grab my sweatpants and throw them on before making my way into the bed.

After a few minutes Ava comes out of the bathroom in her pajamas and lays down facing towards me.

"Good night beautiful," I say as I plant a kiss on her lips.

"Good night."

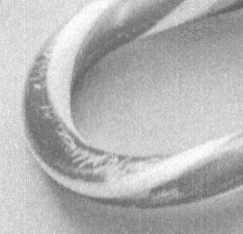

The next morning comes and I wake up in Demetrius's arms. I feel like an ass for ruining the night by crying, but something about him saying we will just spend the weekend together got to me. When he guessed the way I felt about him in the hot tub and him reciprocating the feelings, I figured this would be more than just a weekend thing. I shouldn't let it get to me though because I did invite him here to test out these products and not to start a relationship.

I will say, though, last night went well. I like how we started with something simple to adjust to each other's bodies. The candy cane shaped paddle was interesting because it wasn't like a simple paddle. I did enjoy it along with the tinsel. I will be recommending those go in the lineup when I get back to work.

After sitting and thinking for a few moments, I decide to shimmy my way out of Demetrius's arms because I want some coffee before the day starts. Of course I don't get far before he says, "Good morning beautiful, where do you think you're going?"

I turn to face him and say, "Well a girl needs coffee or you're going to have to deal with the evil side of me."

He begins to laugh. "The evil side? Ava, I doubt you can be evil. You light up any room that you're in."

This man is already being sweet to me, even though I made things awkward last night. I move back over to the bed and pick up one of the pillows before hitting him with it.

"I definitely can be evil," I say with a laugh.

Before I can hit him more with the pillow, he grabs me and pulls me onto his lap.

"Baby girl, you won't hurt a soul. What you need to do is not deflect and actually talk to me about what made you upset last night. I want to be here for you and make you happy, not make you upset."

I don't know what I did to deserve someone like him.

"Look, I might have overreacted. We can dive more into it later today, but when we had the conversation in the hot tub about feelings... I truly meant it when I said I feel something for you. I don't want this to just be a weekend thing, I want it to continue after we leave here."

Instead of him hesitating, he instantly pulls me in for a kiss.

"Ava, if you don't want me to go anywhere then I'm not going anywhere. I'm going to be here by your side until you get tired of me. I think it would be a good idea to really sit down and talk about this and see what happens for us once we leave here, though. How about this... we have a great date today, have fun tonight, and when we head out of here tomorrow afternoon we have a sit down conversation about everything. I don't want to put the stress of what this can be on either of us while we are here having fun. I want you to trust me, though, when I say I want to see where this can go."

I can feel the tears well up in my eyes again. These aren't tears of sadness though, these ones are happiness.

He leans in and wipes the tears from my eyes.

"I'm sorry I'm so emotional. I know this weekend was just supposed to be fun. I didn't mean to let my feelings get the best of me. You truly weren't supposed to know how I feel about you, I wanted to keep it a secret. I wasn't sure if you would reciprocate the feelings and how that would impact with work, but there's just something about you that I love being around."

"Don't make *me* start crying," he says with a laugh.

I instantly reach over and grab the pillow to hit him with it again. Instead of trying to fight me back, he pulls me down to him and plants another kiss on my lips. "Let's go get some coffee."

"Fine, let's go," I say.

We make our way to the kitchen hand in hand, and it turns out Juliana and Collin are already in the kitchen with a pot of coffee ready.

"Good morning, I hope y'all had a great night," Demetrius says.

"Good morning and we did," Collin says as he looks at Juliana with a smirk.

It's still interesting to me that they play it cool like there's nothing really there between them, when there has to be. The tension feels thick between them. One day,

I'm going to get to the bottom of it, but for now I'm shipping the two of them being together.

"Yeah, not too bad of a night. We have to figure out what the plans are for today. Do y'all have anything exciting planned?" Juliana asks.

"We actually haven't figured anything out, but I'm thinking maybe a date by the fireplace tonight," I say as I look over at Demetrius.

"Sounds good to me. Anything on the radar for y'all?" he asks.

Before Juliana can say anything Collin interjects, "I have a date planned for us outside of the cabin."

I can see Juliana's eyes light up with curiosity of what he has planned for the two of them.

"Sure. Just make sure you treat my girl right, or you have another thing coming for you."

"Ava, you know I won't do anything wrong," he says with a slight laugh.

"Good. We're going to go grab a bite to eat and the things we need for tonight," I say.

"Sounds like a plan. If I don't see you before we do, whatever Collin has planned for the two of us, then I will see you in the morning," Juliana says.

"Definitely. Have fun," I say with a smile before we make our way back to our bedroom to get ready.

CHAPTER 15
Demetrius

This morning when Ava told me how she feels about not wanting this to end, I was in total agreement with her. I think it is best to finish out the weekend together then dive more into that when we get home. Today is about spending time together and enjoying each other's company. Since Collin and Juliana are going out for the night, I am determined to make our date night great in the cabin.

"Alright, beautiful. Let's make a list of what we need for tonight. Is there anything in particular you want me to cook for dinner?"

She thinks for a second. "Spaghetti. Sweet and simple, but good."

That's actually easy to make. I jot down a list of what we need.

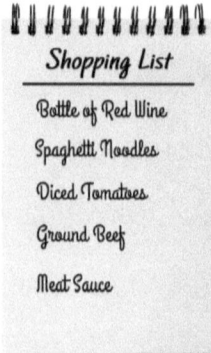

"I can definitely do that. I'm excited to spend the day with you and even more excited to see what we're working with tonight."

"You're not the only one. Let's head to get some food and the groceries we need.

A FEW HOURS GO BY AND WE ARE FINALLY making our way back to the cabin.

We ended up going to one of the local steakhouses for lunch, then went to the store to get everything we needed to make for dinner. When we arrive back at the cabin, I notice that Collin's car is gone. I'm a little shocked they left early, but I'm glad that they are having just as good a time as we are.

It's crazy to think that we have tonight left, then we are heading home. I feel like these past two nights have gone by so fast. I'm happy I was able to pop up to surprise Ava on Thursday, even if it was just to sleep by her side.

When we were talking this morning briefly about how she wants more, it brought me back into my thoughts about how I have been waiting for the right moment to let her know how I feel. We have worked together for the past few years and every time I'm near her I feel a spark inside of me. We've gone out to lunch and hung out outside of work before, but not in this capacity. I truly am grateful that she thought of me to explore the company brands, even if she was hesitant at first.

"Earth to Demetrius. Are we going to get out of the car or sit here all night?" Ava says pulling me out of my thoughts.

"I'm sorry. I got a little lost in my mind."

"Anything you want to tell me?"

"Nope. Just head inside. I will grab all the bags."

She hops out of the car and makes her way to the cabin, looking back before she walks inside. I can see the smile across her face and realization hits me that if I want her, I need to make it known. I don't want to play these childish games. Instead, I want to make her mine. I want to tell her tonight, but I'm going to respect her wishes and wait to bring it up when we get back home tomorrow or on Monday.

I decide I don't want to keep her waiting too long, so I grab the grocery bags and head into the cabin. She's not in the living room. I make my way back to the bedroom and see the most beautiful sight.

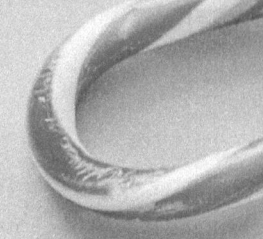

CHAPTER 16
Ava

With the both of us lost in our thoughts, I decide to do something different to spruce up our night.

When I first got here, I noticed there was a holiday themed lingerie set inside the box that I decided to put aside. I've never really been the lingerie type because I know it comes off in a matter of minutes, so it seems pointless to me but tonight there is just something that told me to throw it on to show off my body to Demetrius.

As soon as he told me to head into the cabin, I knew it was the perfect moment to grab the lingerie set and put it on. This outfit doesn't leave much to the imagination. It is crotchless but has bells where my nipples are which is different from what I would normally go for. This might be someone else's style, but it isn't necessarily for me.

Once I slide the outfit on, I stand by the mirror looking over my body. When he walks through the threshold of the bedroom, his eyes instantly light up in a way where he wants to devour me.

"Ava," he begins to say as he makes his way over to me.

Before he can say another word, I instantly kiss him, causing our tongues to intertwine with one another. I can tell I struck a nerve with him because he instantly picks me up and pins me against the nearest wall.

"Baby girl, this wasn't supposed to happen until later tonight. You're making me need you right here, right now."

"Then take me," I whisper into his ear.

While balancing me against the wall, he feels in his pockets to find a condom.

"Fuck, I don't have a condom in my pocket. I need to go grab one," he says.

"Are you clean?"

"I am."

"Then fuck me."

He questions if I'm sure and when I tell him to do it, he instantly maneuvers his sweatpants down his legs while having me still pinned to the wall.

Thank God for these crotchless panties and the fact that I'm already wet for him. He instantly starts to fuck me hard against the wall to the point I'm afraid we're going to break it.

I start to let out a little laugh and he asks, "What's so funny?"

"I think we might break the wall with how hard you're fucking me."

Instead of responding, he pulls me off the wall while

still having me inside of him and slowly maneuvers us over to the bed. He places me down, pulling out of me, and takes his sweatpants off fully before he continues to fuck me. Before he gets to the point where he's going to come, he pulls out and spills his load all over the lingerie set.

"Well, there goes my lingerie piece," I let out another laugh.

"We don't need it anyways. Let's get cleaned up and watch a movie. We can continue the festivities later."

I nod in agreement as we make our way to the shower and clean up after what we just did.

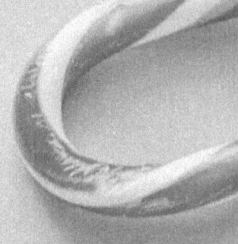

CHAPTER 17
Ava

After our shower we decide to turn on a scary movie to watch until it is time for our makeshift fireplace date.

"What movie are you feeling?" Demetrius asks.

"Hmm, maybe something gory. I don't have a preference."

We end up scrolling through the streaming service platform and end up picking something that appears to fit the gory vibe. Once it starts, I snuggle up closer to him to help with any of the jump scares that there might be. I enjoy scary movies, but sometimes the jump scares get to me.

TWO HOURS LATER, THE MOVIE COMES TO AN end, and I have to say that it is in the top five scary movies

I have watched this year. Shockingly, there weren't too many jump scares in it, so I didn't need Demetrius too much. I will say being cuddled up to him was nice though, especially since it is a little cold in our cabin.

"You ready to make the spaghetti?" I ask.

"Yeah, let's do it. Can you get the pots and pans out while I get the food items we need?"

I nod in agreement as I climb out of the bed.

When we get into the kitchen, I decide to crack open a bottle of red wine to go with the spaghetti. I find two wine glasses and pour each of us a generous glass.

While he begins to cook dinner, I go into the bedroom and set up our fireplace date. I turn the fireplace on, grabbing a blanket, and spread it out on the ground. I look around the room and find the candles that don't require a flame and put them out, too.

Once the room looks set up for our date, I pull out the toys so they are ready for when the time comes. I find Christmas bell nipple clamps and a candy cane vibrator. These are two interesting items that I never imagined myself using. I put them on the nightstand for easy access.

The smell of the meat sauce fills the air and I make my way into the kitchen.

"It smells delicious in here," I say while wrapping my arms around his waist from behind.

He instantly turns to face me and says, "It doesn't smell as delicious as you do."

I can feel my cheeks heat. "You're so corny, but I love it," I say with a laugh.

I enjoy how this man has made me feel these past few days, it's rare that I can find someone who can make me laugh so easily. I am truly glad it has been him and that he took me up on my offer to help me out.

CHAPTER 18
Demetrius

There is just something about Ava that has put a smile on my face the past few days. We have gotten close over the past few years at Lustful Vibe on a professional level, but crossing these boundaries has been nice.

I am excited for our date tonight because we get to stay in and do something here in the cabin. Most people see dates as going somewhere nice, but I think staying in can also be a nice date. This actually allows you to have deeper conversations with someone and have good quality time with them. For me, that is important when I am with someone.

I put two plates of spaghetti with the two glasses of red wine on a tray so it is easy to carry into the bedroom. When I get in the room and see what Ava did to set up, I am in awe. Maybe it is because I have never had a date in front of a fireplace before or maybe something else, I'm not sure.

As I look around the room, my eyes land on the toys that we are to use tonight. I've never used nipple clamps on anyone before, so that looks pretty interesting. The candy cane vibrator also looks perfect because it appears that it provides vaginal and clitoral stimulation. I will know for sure later when we test it out, though. For now, I draw my attention to her and the date in front of us.

"I love this vibe you have brought together. Everything feels so nice and cozy."

"Thank you. I can't wait to try your spaghetti and see how it tastes," she says.

I bring the tray down to the floor before lowering myself onto the ground.

"Let's dig in. I do hope you like it."

She lowers herself down to sit across from me. "I'm sure I will enjoy every bit of it and dessert, too."

A smirk comes across my face. She will definitely be my dessert tonight, but that's going to have to wait.

AFTER AVA AND I FINISH EATING SHE DECIDES to lay her head across my lap while looking up at the ceiling.

"Thank you for coming. Not just to help me with the company project, but to spend genuine time with me. I feel like that's hard to come by sometimes," she says while looking up.

"Baby girl, I'm glad you invited me here. I know it's only been a few days, but I have enjoyed every moment I have been able to spend with you. I know we have to leave tomorrow, but I don't want this to be the last time we spend together outside of work. If you would let me, I would like to make this a regular occasion. You have such a great vibe, so I want to learn more about who Ava is outside of work."

I can tell she is contemplating what I said because it takes a moment for her to respond. "Are you sure that's what you want?"

I tilt her head back so she is looking directly at me. "Of course that's what I want. Don't think you're getting rid of me just yet."

I can tell that sparked something in her because she sits up and moves over to straddle my lap.

"Well then, yes, I would love to see where this leads after we leave the cabin," she says as she leans in to kiss me.

"Let me go grab the toys so they are nearby for when we need them."

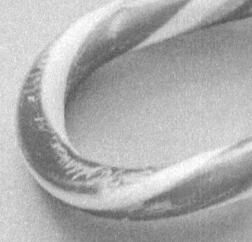

CHAPTER 19
Ava

W hen Demetrius comes back with the toys, I instantly devour him. I don't know what has gotten into me, but I have been so horny when I'm around him. I can't imagine what it will be like when we aren't in this space, and we are back home. I'm sure it will be even better.

We begin ripping our clothes off like animals. *Good thing the fireplace is here to keep us warm.* This moment feels so heated like we need to attack one another. Every movement is quick and before I know it, we're both naked.

"You ready to have some fun?" Demetrius asks.

Instead of answering him, I decide to show him instead.

I lower myself so my face is aligned with his dick. I slowly take him into my mouth where I learn this was probably a mistake—he is so big, I'm afraid I'm going to choke on him. I love how he isn't being forceful with me and is letting me suck him off on my terms.

I take him in and out of my mouth while gently squeezing on his balls causing him to moan out. I pick up the speed and before I know it he is tapping my shoulder as a sign that he is about to cum. Instead of pulling him out of my mouth, I pick up the speed until cum starts to shoot down my throat causing me to drink him down.

"Fuck, Ava. That was amazing."

"I try," I say with a laugh.

He lays me down on the blanket and brings his face down to my pussy. He begins to lick and suck at my clit before grabbing the toys. "That was just a warm-up. Let's see how your body does with these."

He begins to attach the clamps to each of my nipples and tugs gently which sends a chill through my body. *I see how those work then, but I'm not sure if I like them.*

"We will come back to using these. It's my first time, so hopefully I will do something right with them."

"Yeah, let's do that because I don't really know how I feel about them right now. It kinda hurts, but at the same time it feels good."

"I get that. I don't want to cause you pain, unless it's going to bring you pleasure."

He goes to grab the candy cane vibrator and slowly pushes it into me with the end of the candy cane pressed upon my clit. It slowly buzzes to life and it feels amazing.

"Fuck, Demetrius. This feels so good," I moan out.

I can feel the vibration on both my clit and my G-spot which is sending my body to the edge.

Demetrius slowly pulls on the nipple clamps which sets my body into overdrive. There is just something about the way all of these different components feel on my body that has me ready to cum.

Before I know it, I feel Demtrius's tongue along my clit.

"Fuck," I moan.

"Baby girl, I hope you enjoy all the pleasure I'm bringing to you," he says in between licks.

Boy, do I enjoy this.

He picks up his pace before sending me over that edge, causing my legs to shake uncontrollably. I can feel a wet substance shoot out of me, and I become embarrassed.

"I love the way you squirt for me," he says as he brings his mouth to mine. We deepen our kiss while he removes the toy from my pussy. I feel like I'm at a loss for words. "Are you ready for me to fuck you like the good girl that you are?" he asks.

Shit, that does something to me.

I like the praise. Maybe that's going to be a new kink for me.

"How about you stop talking and just fuck me."

It's like he has been waiting for me to say that because he instantly aligns himself with my entrance and starts to fuck me nice and slow.

"Harder please," I let out.

I feel like I shouldn't have said that because he fucks me harder while pulling on my nipple clamps. I can feel the pain mixed with pleasure as the bells make noise with every thrust. As he buries himself deeper into me, I can feel another orgasm coming over me.

"You feel amazing, baby girl."

This causes him to pick up his pace until my pussy clenches around him as I cum. A few seconds later, he pulls out and shoots out his release onto my stomach.

"Let's go wash off these activities from the day, pack, and relax in bed until it's time to head to bed since we have to leave tomorrow," he says as he gently pulls the nipple clamps off.

"I'm down," I say as I grab his hand and escort him into the shower.

I turn the water up onto one of the hotter settings as we get inside. I don't know what has gotten into me, but I don't want this night to end. I lower myself where my mouth is aligned with his dick and slowly bring him into my mouth.

"You don't have to do this," he says.

"I want to," I say as I take him in and out of my mouth. I continue until he begins to cum again.

I release him with a pop before washing and grabbing a towel, a smirk on my face at his dazed look. Once we're back in the bedroom, I laugh, saying, "I don't know how you cum so much, I don't think I could do it."

He just shakes his head at me. "Maybe it's just something about you that has me turned on and coming so easily."

This makes me blush because I don't really know what's good about me for another person to find interest in me.

He draws me from my thoughts and lifts my head up to face him. "Ava, don't get in your feelings, I have enjoyed every part of this experience thus far. Although we have to go home tomorrow, don't think this is going to be the last time you see me out of work."

"When I see it, I will believe it."

"Well, you will. We can navigate this when we head out tomorrow," he says while planting a kiss on my lips.

"Alright. Goodnight."

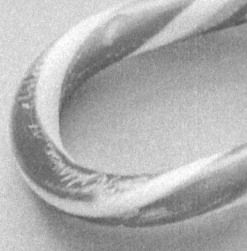

CHAPTER 20
Ava
SUNDAY, DECEMBER 23, 2025

The next morning comes and I am rudely awakened to a loud noise on my phone. I look down and see it is 7 a.m. There is a notification on my phone that says "EMERGENCY WEATHER ALERT. HEAVY SNOWFALL IS OCCURRING IN YOUR AREA. STAY INDOORS."

Fuck, we need to get out of here.

I look to my side and see Demetrius looking at his phone, too.

"I think we should go downstairs and see the others to say our goodbyes so we can get indoors before the snow starts to fall harder," I say.

"Yeah, I agree. Let's go," Demetrius expresses.

We head to the kitchen where Collin and Juliana are already present.

"Did y'all see the alert?" Juliana asks.

"Yeah we did. I think we should get our bags together and get out of here before the snowfall gets to the point where we're trapped. It's so close to Christmas and I don't want to be stuck here, even if I do love you," I say with my attention directed to Juliana.

"I agree, let's get packed up. I will see y'all at work on Wednesday" Collin says while shaking Demetrius's hand and bringing me in for a hug.

"I will see y'all at work," I say as I hug both of them goodbye.

Demetrius and I head back into the bedroom and get all of our items packed up to leave the cabin. I look out the window and see the snow starting to fall harder.

"Looks like we need to hurry about and get out of here. Do you want to come back to my house? No pressure." I am a little embarrassed that I blurted that out. I don't know why I would think that he would want to come back with me.

"I need to stop by my house to grab some more clothes, then I can come over and hang out. I don't know what the weather might bring, so I want to be prepared."

Yes, I'm so glad he is coming back with me. Granted we do have two more toys to test out.

"Perfect, I will text you my address."

After getting everything packed up, we make our way to our cars. Demetrius helps me load my bags in the car and plants a kiss on my head as he heads home. I instantly send him a text so he has my address.

Me: 1721 Hungerford Street

Demetrius: Got it. See you soon, baby girl.

Ahh, I love the nickname he has for me. It makes me

happy because it's something that we share between the two of us. and I don't really know why.

AFTER DRIVING FOR A LITTLE WHILE, I AM finally pulling into the driveway of my home. The snow is definitely coming down which made me have to drive a little slower than I normally would. I hope Demetrius will be able to come over still.

Once I get into the house, I look at my phone and see a text message from him.

> Demetrius: I just got to my house. I will leave shortly and be at your house within the next thirty minutes.

Thirty minutes is going to take forever. Instead of sitting and counting down the time, I make some hot chocolate. With the weather outside, this is perfect to have right now.

I head into the living room and light my peppermint and pine candle to get the house smelling like Christmas, deciding to find a show to watch while I wait.

About halfway through the show, I hear my doorbell go off. To be on the safe side, I look through the peephole and notice it's Demetrius so I let him in.

"How was the drive? It looks like the snow is coming down more than it was when we left the cabin."

"It wasn't bad. Luckily I have four-wheel drive, so I

don't have to worry about it too much. I did pick up some breakfast since we had to get out of the cabin quickly."

"Thank you. You didn't have to do that."

"I know I didn't have to, but I wanted to," he says as he places a kiss on the top of my head before placing the bag of food on the table.

"This definitely looks delicious."

We continue to make small talk as we eat, while still avoiding the conversation of what is going to happen next for us.

CHAPTER 21

Demetrius

As we were leaving the cabin this morning, my brain kept flowing with different thoughts about Ava. I was a little nervous for what was to come once we left, but having her invite me over makes me feel better.

Seeing the way she lit up with my presence when I walked through the front door is something I could get used to. I know we have two more toys to test out today, so I want to bring the focus onto that rather than our feelings for one another.

"So, do you want to go test these toys out now or later?" she asks.

I can't help but laugh because I thought we would spend a little time together before we just jump into that, but if she's down then I'm down, too.

"I mean if you're ready to, then let's do this."

She grabs my hand and escorts me back to where her bedroom is. For living by herself, it is pretty spacious here. I wonder if she ever gets lonely being here alone. At least for today she has me here with her.

I can tell she is already good to go because she pulls the toys out of her bag and begins to attack my face with hers. I pick her up while intertwining my tongue with hers. I can feel my dick straining against my pants with the way our bodies are interacting with one another. I lay her across the bed and pull down her panties and pants before I instantly devour her center.

"Your pussy is so wet for me. Have you been thinking about this?"

She moans. "Yes."

I look beside me and determine which toy I want to use first. I decide the candy cane glass butt plug is a good place to start, but I need to warm up her ass up first. I pull away from her center so I can talk her through how the butt plug is going to go.

"Alright, baby girl. This first toy is going to be a butt plug. I'm going to put plenty of lube on it, but I want you to be calm and relax your muscles, so it doesn't hurt going in. This is going to make you feel full. We're going to start slowly with getting your body adjusted to it, then we will move it around so you can get the full effect of it. Remember, you have your safe word if you need to use it if things become a bit too much."

I can see her start to relax as I'm explaining how the interaction is going to go.

"Okay, I'm ready. I have seen how butt plugs work before," she says as she leans in to kiss me.

I grab the lube and ensure the butt plug has plenty on it, while also placing some lube on her asshole.

"Okay, I'm going to be gentle. Prepare yourself."

She nods in agreement as I start to slowly insert the butt plug into her.

"This feels so weird."

"Is that a good or a bad weird?"

She hesitates for a second. "I think it's a good weird if that makes any sense."

"It makes total sense, it's a new feeling for you. I'm going to slowly move it in and out of you, so if it feels like it's becoming too much then use that safe word."

I begin to move the butt plug in and out her ass, causing her to moan with pleasure. Since I can tell she is enjoying herself, I add the other toy. This one is a vibrator in the shape of a Santa hat that makes a flicking motion on the clit.

I pair the two toys together and I can see her body go into overload with the different feelings.

"Fuck Demetrius, this is too much."

"Call your safe word if you want me to stop."

She continues to moan in pleasure. "I'm not doing that, I want this."

I begin to pick up the pace with the plug, and it causes her body to come undone.

"Demetrius," she yells out as she comes.

"You good, baby girl?"

"Hell yes. You should definitely fuck me now."

"Nope. I want today to be about you and the way that you're feeling. I'm going to draw you a bath with the gingerbread bubble bath I got from the store. Your body definitely needs rest, since it's been through so much the past few days."

"Okay," she says with disappointment in her eyes.

I lean in to kiss her. "Trust me. You need the rest."

I make my way into the bathroom and see that she has a jacuzzi bathtub that's separate from the shower. I turn the water up to ensure that it is warm enough before adding the bubble bath to it.

"Go relax in the tub. I'm going to hop in the shower."

She comes closer to me. "No, you're not. You're coming to get in the bath with me."

There's no arguing with this woman, so I do as she says. I strip out of my clothes and make my way into the bathroom first. She comes in and positions herself where her back is pressed against my chest.

Shit, I could get used to this.

"You comfortable?" I ask.

"Yeah, I am. Are you?"

"Yup, just fine."

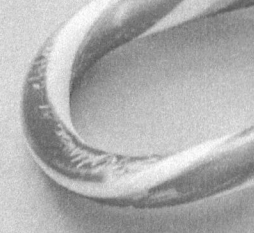

CHAPTER 22
Ava

Being in the bathtub with Demetrius makes me feel a way that is hard to explain. I've never been in this predicament before with someone else, so it is nice to be cuddled up.

He begins to rub along my shoulders with the loofah. "What are you thinking about, baby girl?"

It's like he is a mind reader because he seems to know just when I'm thinking about things.

"I'm just thinking about how things feel so different with you so far. I don't know if it's because we've had a close work relationship, then this happened or what."

"Don't overthink things. We have had a great weekend thus far, and like I told you before, we can figure out where we want things to go from here. Right now, just relax, and lean into me."

Even though that's harder said than done, I lay back and close my eyes for a few minutes.

After being in the bathtub for twenty minutes or so, we decide to hop in the shower to clean off the day's festivities. I know it's still early, but I'm getting a little tired after everything that has happened.

Once we are done, I throw on a pajama set Before saying, "Do you want to lay in bed and watch some movies for the rest of the night, or are you heading home?"

"I want to stay, if you'll let me."

"I would like that. It's kinda like when you see couples in movies spending the night together when the snow is falling... minus the couple part."

He looks at me like he wants to say something, but he hesitates and puts his clothes on instead.

We both climb into the bed and watch a few movies before I fall fast asleep on his chest.

CHAPTER 23
Demetrius

MONDAY, DECEMBER 24, 2025

I wake up to see Ava fast asleep, cuddled up to me. I don't know how she went to bed early and slept through the night, but she did. I wish I could get sleep like that but my brain was running all night about how I wanted things to go for today and on Christmas.

I planned to stay through both days, then head into work with her on Wednesday. I don't want her thinking that I just came for the weekend, and that was it.

A few months ago, I came across this charm bracelet that has sunflowers on it. Sunflowers are one of her favorite flowers, so I knew I had to get them for her. I was waiting until Christmas time to give it to her as a way to show not only my appreciation for her, but also my interest in her. I'm a little nervous about how she is going to feel about it, but what better way than finding out while we're together for the holiday.

While Ava continues to sleep, I slide out of bed and make my way to the kitchen. I have no idea what she has in the fridge and freezer, but I hope there's something in here for me to make her breakfast in bed. As soon as I open the fridge I see eggs, but that's about it.

If I was thinking about it, I could've grabbed something on my way here.

I guess I will have to make the eggs do. It appears that she has some orange juice and bread too, so I can pair them together for her. I quickly scramble up the eggs and put them on a plate.

Carrying the plate of food and orange juice to the room, I say in a soft tone, "Ava, wake up."

She appears groggy at first as she tries to wake herself up. "Good morning," she says with sleepiness in her tone still.

"Good morning, baby girl. I made you some eggs and toast. You really don't have much in your fridge, but I wanted to make you something to get your day started."

"You're a sweetie. Nobody has ever made me breakfast in bed before, so I'm thankful to have this from you."

"Well, get used to it because it's going to happen more often than not."

I can tell she looks a little confused and hesitant on what she should say in return.

"About that... I think we need to sit and talk about that today. I want to be on the same page about everything, especially with what happened this weekend between us. I know it was for fun but—" she starts to say before I interrupt her.

"But you should eat your food, then when you get out of bed we can talk more about it."

"Alright," she says as she starts to make a sandwich with the toast and eggs.

"That's one way to make it. I wish you had some bacon because that would have been a good sandwich all together."

"I know. I keep telling myself I need to go shopping, but I never made it that far. It's all good though, I will do that this upcoming weekend."

"Yeah, you might need to do that. I'm going to head out to the living room, when you're done eating I will see you out here."

She nods in agreement as she takes her next bite from the sandwich.

CHAPTER 24
Ava

Waking up to breakfast in bed was something completely unexpected, but I definitely can get used to it.

Once I finish eating, I decide to stay in my pajamas and head out to the living room where Demetrius is sitting on the couch. He has one of my favorite Christmas movies up on the screen for us to watch, but I think it's important to address the elephant in the room first.

"Thank you again for breakfast, it was delicious."

"Don't thank me," he says as he comes to kiss my head.

"So, is it time to have that conversation now about what the next steps are going to look like for us? I don't want things to be weird when we go back to work, so I want to ensure we are on the same page with everything. If you want the past few days to have just been a work assignment, then it can be that."

"Please don't think I want this to just be a work

assignment. Ava, I have had feelings for you for the last six months, but I have been too much of a coward to come out and tell you how I feel. I want you to know that when you told me about the task you were assigned by Benjamin, that I wanted you to ask me to be involved. I knew this opportunity would open up doors for me to tell you how I feel about you. I don't want this to have just been a weekend where we fucked and walked away like nothing happened. I want to test this thing out between the two of us. I want to show you the world and what you should deserve to feel."

I feel tears well up in my eyes with his words.

"I'm sorry if I'm a bit emotional. I have been wanting to experience these real feelings with someone for such a long time, but I was never able to have them. With my ex-boyfriend, he hated me when he found out that I was going to work for Lustful Vibe. He couldn't accept the reasons why I took this job, so seeing you in the position that you are in for the company instantly drew me to you. I saw that you were the type of person that is open to the sex toy industry. Every day that I work with you and go over sales and get closer to you, I am drawn in more and more. I really don't want to lose that or ruin our friendship."

"Baby girl, we are not going to ruin our friendship. At the end of the day, that's what comes first. We have built a foundation as friends, and I refuse to let that slip away from me. I want to be with you and give this a real shot. What are you thinking right now?"

What am I thinking? Shoot, maybe that I'm not

good enough. Maybe that things will be awkward between the two of us. I don't know.

"I just want to ensure that we are making the right decision."

"I think we're making the right decision. How about this, we give it a shot. If it works, then we can be happy together. If it doesn't work, then we agree to just be friends again."

I reach out my hand, so we can shake on it. "That sounds like a plan to me."

He shakes my hand back. "Will you be my girlfriend, Ava Taylor?"

I get really excited and pull him in for a hug saying, "Of course I will."

We bring each other in for an embrace and interlock our tongues with one another.

"Hey, hey. Let's not get too carried away. My favorite movie is on the TV screen, so let's go watch it."

"Fine, let's go," he says.

CHAPTER 25

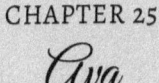

Ava

A few hours later, we finish up our movie. I head to the window and see the snow covering the driveway and the bushes outside. *Demetrius definitely isn't going anywhere, even if he wanted to.*

"Alright boyfriend... what do you want to do next?" I ask while looking at the clock and seeing that it's only 3 p.m., so we have all night.

"I'm down for whatever you want to do. It's Christmas Eve so we can just hang out the rest of the day and watch Christmas movies if you would like. You can also show me how to make that mulled wine you enjoy."

"That sounds like a great way to spend the rest of the night with you. Making the mulled wine is super easy, let's go in the kitchen and I can show you."

When we get to the kitchen I pull out the crockpot, a bottle of red wine, mulling spices, and crabapple juice.

"It's only three ingredients?" he asks with confusion on his face.

"Yeah, it's sweet and simple. You just have to ensure

you use red wine. We're going to throw it in the crockpot and let it cook on low to get it warm before it's ready. I would say it can take about thirty minutes to an hour."

"This really doesn't seem bad at all. I think I can make this next time."

"Good because I don't feel like making it all the time," I say with a laugh.

While we wait for the mulled wine to get warm, we continue chatting about what we want our relationship to look like. I'm glad we both value honesty and communication within a relationship. That is something I believe makes or breaks one. If two people can't be honest, then it makes the relationship challenging.

About 45 minutes later, the mulled wine is finally done. Demetrius grabs us two coffee mugs from one of the cabinets and pours some of the wine in each cup.

"Mmh, this is so delicious," he says as he takes a sip.

"Told you, you would like it. Now let's go lay in bed and watch movies and chat for the night. I would say let's fuck, but my holes are still a little sore," I say with a laugh.

"Yeah, we definitely need to rest those up because tomorrow, I'm going to devour every inch of your body as we celebrate Christmas together."

With that, we head back into the bedroom, turn the TV on, and chat a little more about our feelings and why we were both afraid to confess how we felt about one another.

CHAPTER 26

Demetrius

TUESDAY, DECEMBER 25, 2025

Today is going to be a good day, I can feel it. I can't wait to give Ava the bracelet and see if she likes it. I'm sure she will based on all the sunflower decorations she has both at work and in her home.

I decide to start this day off with a bang.

"Good morning, Ava," I say while planting a kiss on her head.

Her response is inaudible until she finally sits up out of the bed.

"Merry Christmas, beautiful."

"Merry Christmas to you, too," she says as she leans in for a kiss.

"I could get used to waking up to you every day, but I don't want to rush things. Later today, I'm going to head home and get ready for work in the morning."

I can see the sadness come across her face.

"Are you sure you have to go today? Can you please stay tonight," she says with puppy dog eyes.

"Baby girl, I wish I could but all my items for work are at home."

"Boo, I guess you need to make it up to me for you leaving me tonight."

"Don't need to tell me twice," I say while moving her where she is positioned underneath me.

I slowly pull her clothes off her causing her nipples to harden from the coldness in the room. I lower myself down the bed where my face is positioned right with her center. I can see the anticipation on her face, so I begin to slowly lick her clit.

"Fuck Demetrius, stop being a tease."

She's going to regret saying that because she's about to get destroyed by my mouth, fingers, and dick.

I pick up the pace with my tongue, getting her nice and wet before I insert two fingers inside of her, making a 'come here' motion, which causes her legs to begin to tremble. Her moans get louder and right as I feel her walls begin to clench, I pull my fingers out.

"Hey! That's not fair."

"How about you flip over so your stomach is laying on the bed and your ass is in the air."

She does what I say and seeing that beautiful ass of her has me turned on even more. Since we still have the lube nearby, I take some lube and put it onto her ass.

I line my dick up with her pretty pussy and begin to pound inside of her, while taking my thumb and sticking it in her ass.

"Fuck, I feel so full. Please don't stop."

I continue to pound into her deeper and faster to the point where she's screaming out my name as she comes.

"I'm about to come," I say as I continue to stroke her a few more times.

Right before I reach my climax, I can feel her pussy clenching around me. I instantly pull out and cum all over her back. I slowly pull my finger out of her ass and go to the bathroom to grab a washcloth to clean her up.

She rolls onto her back and says, "Well damn, I know not to call you a tease again."

"I bet you do know to not call me that again."

She pulls me back into the bed with her and we lay there side by side naked.

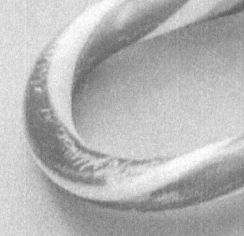

CHAPTER 27
Ava

Demetrius knows how to fuck a woman. I loved the part where he decided to stick a finger in my ass. It made my senses go on overdrive and caused me to easily orgasm. I definitely want him to do that again.

We lay here in the bed together and I contemplate what I want to do next, so instead I decide to talk to him.

"Thank you for showing me a good time and making this work assignment actually enjoyable."

"I am always here if you need something from me. Let's go get cleaned up, I have a surprise for you."

A surprise? I have no idea what that could be. We really didn't plan anything for the weekend and definitely didn't talk about doing any gift exchanges.

"Don't be worried. I'm sure you will like it," he says as he grabs my hand and escorts me into the shower.

We spent about twenty minutes in the shower where we proceeded to have another round of sex. It felt good to be able to clean each other up. Although we are staying in for the rest of the night, I still decide to throw on a red sweater with some black pants to make myself a little festive for the holiday. Demetrius opts for a green long-sleeve shirt with black pants, too.

We head to the living room and I notice he has a black box on the coffee table, waiting for me to open it. I have no idea how he got this out here without me seeing it.

He makes his way to the box and hands it out to me. "I hope you like it."

Nerves build inside of me because I have no idea what it could be.

When I open it, I can feel some of the tears drip down my eyes—there is a sunflower bracelet in the box. This is my favorite flower, and it shows that he paid attention to that.

"It's beautiful. Can you put it on me?" I ask.

I hand him the bracelet and he clasps it around my wrist in one swift motion. It fits perfectly.

"Thank you so much for the gift. I'm sorry I didn't get you anything. I didn't really plan to be in this situation."

"Please don't apologize. I've had it for months and was looking for the right time to give it to you. All that matters is that you like it."

"Of course I do," I say while planting a kiss on his lips.

This really is turning out to be the best Christmas ever.

We spend a little more time together before we have to say our goodbyes for the night. I really don't want him to leave, but I understand why he has to.

"I will see you tomorrow," he says while pulling me in for a hug.

"Please text me when you get home."

"I will."

We exchange a kiss and he makes his way home.

I HEAR MY PHONE PING AND SEE IT'S DEMETRIUS.

> Demetrius: I made it home safely

Me: Good. What's next?

> Demetrius: I'm going to chill and probably head to bed in an hour or two. Wbu?

Me: I wish you could have stayed but I know you couldn't. I'm just going to watch some reality TV and head to bed in a little bit, too.

My phone starts to ring and see it's a video call from Demetrius.

"Did you miss my face already?" I question.

"Of course I did."

We continue to chat on video for the next couple hours about everything and anything, then realize it's time to head to bed.

"I'm sad, but it looks like I need to get ready to head

to bed. I will see you in the morning at work. Maybe you can meet Benjamin with me for my review?"

"I will be wherever you need me to be."

"Perfect. Good night, Demetrius."

"Good night, baby girl." With that we hang up.

I get ready for bed and drift off into a slumber.

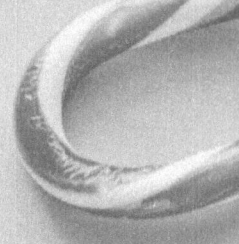

CHAPTER 28

Ava

WEDNESDAY, DECEMBER 26, 2025

The next morning comes and my alarm wakes me up at 7 a.m. sharp. I have to be at work by 8 a.m., so I go through my normal morning routine to get there on time.

Once I'm done getting myself together, I see a text from Demetrius.

> **Demetrius:** Good morning, beautiful. I can't wait to see you and tell everyone you're mine.

> **Me:** Good morning, babe. Slow it down, the boss has to know first 😂

> **Demetrius:** I'm sorry. I just want the world to know you're mine.

> **Me:** They will know sooner rather than later. I have to finish getting ready, but I'll see you in a little bit.

> **Demetrius:** I will see you soon 😘

I don't know what I did to deserve this man. From the moment he told me his feelings, he has really made me feel supported and cared for. I'm thankful to have him by my side.

After I'm done getting ready for work, I make my short drive into the office. When I arrive, I see Demetrius waiting outside of his car for me.

It's too damn cold for that.

"Good morning again," he says as he leans in to plant a kiss on my lips.

"Morning." I kiss him back.

I really want to grab his hand and walk in holding it, but I know we need to tell Benjamin about the relationship first. Demetrius and I had a great conversation about our relationship and boundaries to set at work last night, so we know what we're walking into today.

We head into the office and I drop all my bags off at my desk, before I go through my usual routine of making a coffee. As I make my way to the office kitchen, I see Juliana at her desk so I stop by.

"Good morning, girl! I hope you had a wonderful weekend?"

"I did, I hope you did, too? How's things with Demetrius?" she asks.

"Things are going really well, we decided to make things official. How about you and Collin?"

I can see excitement fill her when I tell her I'm officially off the market.

"I'm so happy for you. The story about Collin is one for another time. Go grab your coffee and I will chat with you about it later," she says with a laugh.

"Yes ma'am. I hope your visit with Benjamin goes well, too."

After grabbing my coffee, I make my way to Benjamin's office where he is sitting behind his desk like he was waiting for one of us to come meet with him.

"Come, sit. How was your weekend?" he asks as I walk in and shut the door behind me.

"The weekend went well. I do want to just start off by saying thank you for the opportunity to test out the products. During that time, I invited Demetrius and we made the decision to officially date."

"It's about damn time," Benjamin says while letting out a laugh. I know he can see the confusion spread across my face. "Sorry for my language, but I knew that was going to happen. I think y'all were just oblivious to the connection that y'all had, but I'm glad to hear things are working out with y'all. Besides that, how were the products?"

He pulls out an evaluation check-list that has my items and toys listed:

☐ **TINSEL FOR BONDAGE**

☐ **CANDY CANE PADDLE**

☐ **CANDY CANE VIBRATOR**

☐ **SANTA HAT VIBRATOR**

☐ **CANDY CANE GLASS BUTT PLUG**

☐ **CHRISTMAS BELL NIPPLE CLAMPS**

☐ **CHRISTMAS THEMED LINGERIE**

"Well, that's a loaded question. There were definitely items that I had to adjust to. The tinsel served its purpose for bondage, but I feel like some other type of restraint would be better. The only product that I wasn't a fan of was the Christmas Bell Nipple Clamps. I personally didn't like the way they felt on my nipples, but that doesn't mean someone else might not like it. I think it's an acquired feeling."

He looks deep in thought about the responses.

"Do you have something else you would like to see in place of the tinsel?"

"I'm thinking some type of rope-based item because if I wanted to get out of the tinsel I could have."

"Okay, that's something good for me to know. Is there any other feedback that you want me to know?"

"Uh I don't think so. The products were definitely couple friendly. I'm sure they can also be used individually, but I think most of them would be best used together."

I can see him jotting down notes as I'm talking.

"We can definitely make a note of that and see if we can get some more products that can be used individually as well."

"Perfect. I think having a variety is important because not everyone has a partner."

"That's a good point. I do want to say thank you and Demetrius for being willing to try out these products, including the ones you didn't really enjoy. I would like to offer you both a week's worth of paid vacation to a destination of your choosing."

I let out a mini scream. I didn't expect this at all, but I'm so glad that I'll get to spend more time with him away from here.

"Thank you so much. We will definitely let you know where we want to go so we can plan that for next year."

CHAPTER 29
Ava

After my meeting with Benjamin, my first stop is to tell Demetrius about what happened. I make my way over to his desk which is only located a few over from mine.

He sees me coming up. "Hey babe, how did the meeting go?"

"It went better than I expected. He already had a feeling about us and our relationship. He is completely on board and figured that our relationship would happen sooner rather than later."

"That's a good thing then. It didn't seem like you were in there for a long time."

"Nope. He had a checklist of the items we had and I gave him my honest feedback. If there are any thoughts you have about them, then you can let him know, too."

"I'm sure you told him everything that he needed to know based on our conversation we had last night."

"Perfect. I do want to say that he offered us a week's

paid vacation together, so we need to figure out what we want to do for that."

I can see the shock come across his face like I'm telling him a fib.

"Are you being serious?"

"Dead ass."

He stands up and brings me up for a hug.

"I'm so excited to go on this vacation with you and get to spend more time with you somewhere outside of the states," he says.

"I'm so happy to do that too. I can't wait to see where life takes us," I say with a smile.

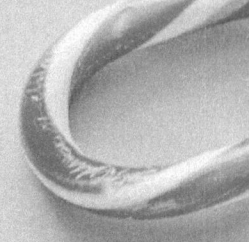

Epilogue: Ava
TWO MONTHS LATER

These past few months with Demetrius have been wonderful. I was very hesitant at first about where things would lead us, but I'm glad they ended up working out.

We both decided we don't want to rush the things that happen in our relationship, so we haven't talked about moving in with one another or anything like that. Instead, we will rotate weekends at each other's home. This allows us to still spend time together but also have time apart.

Overall, our relationship has been healthy. I was able to win an award for number one salesperson at Lustful Vibe which has been such a blessing because I didn't expect it to happen. Benjamin was also able to implement my feedback on the Christmas themed products, which was good to see as well.

I love how I always have a voice within this company. I also love how supportive Benjamin has continued to be in our relationship. Juliana has continued to be my best friend. I feel like the cabin trip was able to bring us closer than we ever were before, so I'm thankful for that, too. I have also been able to get to know Collin more.

After thinking about everything going on and the successes I have had, I decide to head over to Demetrius's house. I ring the doorbell and he is already at the front door with a cup of mulled wine in hand for me.

"Hey, baby," he says, handing me the cup.

I take a sip. "This is actually pretty good. Look at you learning a little something. Shows you pay attention to me sometimes."

We both start laughing. I love this aspect of our relationship because we are always having a good time and are able to laugh together.

He moves out of my way so I can go into the house, where I head straight to the couch and get comfortable.

"I've been thinking a lot recently..." I begin to say.

"Oh no, I hope you haven't been thinking of anything bad."

"No, nothing bad at all. What I was thinking about is where we should take that paid vacation."

"Well, if we go in a couple weeks, then it will be warm outside. Do you have any top contenders of where you want to go?"

"How about a cruise?"

"I've never been on one, but I'd be down to do it."

This makes me giddy inside because I haven't been on one either, but I've been dying to go.

"Let's do it, then."

Acknowledgments

To my alpha readers (Emma, Hilary & Lo), thank you for always reading the books I throw at you and helping me spruce them up for others to get.

To my readers, thank you so much for picking up my books and supporting me while I go on this rollercoaster of a journey as an author.

Kpknupp thank you for helping me rework some components of my story and brainstorm company and character names.

Ava Wylde, Licia Dawn, Layla Douglas, Emily Klepp, and Jamie Fritz... Thank y'all for being my author friends and listening to me while I go through different ideas and mini rants. I appreciate each and every one of you for your support too.

About the Author

Deann Soleil is a self-published author based in Virginia who focuses on writing forbidden romances. When not writing, she is a full-time social worker who works with victims of community violence to help them overcome their traumatic experiences. If you're looking for short, fast-paced books, then look no further.

Also by Deann Soleil

Consumed by the Professor

Chasing the Forbidden Desire

Stalked Through the Night

A Twisted Thanksgiving Holiday

Anthologies:

A Wild Run Anthology (The Chase)

Monsters, Masks & Mayhem Anthology (The Graveyard)

Christmas Temptation Anthology (One Stop at Love)